A BARGAIN
FOR
FRANCES

HarperFestival®
A Division of HarperCollins*Publishers*

A BARGAIN FOR FRANCES

by Russell Hoban
Pictures by Lillian Hoban

HarperCollins®, 🅖®, HarperFestival®, and An I Can Read Picture Book™
are trademarks of HarperCollins Publishers Inc.

A Bargain for Frances
Text copyright © 1970, renewed 1998, Russell C. Hoban
Illustrations copyright © 1970, renewed 1998, Estate of Lillian Hoban
Revised illustrations copyright © 1992, Estate of Lillian Hoban
Printed in the U.S.A. All rights reserved.
http://www.harperchildrens.com

Library of Congress Cataloging-in-Publication Data
Hoban, Russell.
    A bargain for Frances / by Russell Hoban ; pictures by Lillian Hoban.
        p.   cm. — (An I can read picture book)
    Summary: Frances foils Thelma's plot to trick her out of a new china set.
    ISBN 0-694-01295-5
    [1. Badgers—Fiction.   2. Friendship—Fiction.]   I. Hoban, Lillian, ill.   II. Title.   III. Series.
PZ7.H627Bar   1999   98-47659
[E]—dc21   CIP
                                                                                                                  AC

Typography by Gene Vosough and David Horowitz
1   2   3   4   5   6   7   8   9   10
❖
First An I Can Read Picture Book edition, 1999

For Phoebe, Brom, Esmé, and Julia

It was a fine summer day, and after
breakfast Frances said, "I am going to play
with Thelma."

"Be careful," said Mother.

"Why do I have to be careful?" said Frances.

"Remember the last time?" said Mother.

"Which time was that?" said Frances.

"That was the time you played catch with Thelma's new boomerang," said Mother. "Thelma did all the throwing, and you came home with lumps on your head."

"I remember that time now," said Frances.

"And do you remember the other time last winter?" said Mother.

"I remember that time too," said Frances. "That was the first time there was ice on the pond. Thelma wanted to go skating, and she told me to try the ice first."

"Who came home wet?" said Mother. "You or Thelma?"

"I came home wet," said Frances.

"Yes," said Mother. "That is why I say be careful. Because when you play with Thelma you always get the worst of it."

"Well," said Frances, "this time I do not have to be careful. We are not playing with boomerangs. We are not skating. We are having a tea party, and we are making a mud cake."

"Be careful anyhow," said Mother.

"All right," said Frances.

Frances took her dolls to Thelma's house. She took her alligator doll and her elephant doll. She took her snake doll and her teddy bear too.

As Frances walked to Thelma's house she sang:

> *Alligators, bears and me*
>
> *Are very fond of drinking tea.*
>
> *The elephant and the wiggly snake*
>
> *Are happy when they eat their cake.*

Frances and Thelma made a mud cake.
They put daisies on it for frosting. Then
Thelma got out her dolls and her tea set.

"I am saving up for a tea set," said Frances.

"I am saving all my allowances."

"This is the best kind to get," said Thelma.

"It is plastic, and it has red flowers on it."

"This is not the kind I want," said Frances. "I want a real china tea set with pictures on it in blue. The tea set I want has trees and birds and a Chinese house and a fence and a boat and people walking on a bridge. I used to have that kind of tea set. But all I have now is part of the teapot. The rest of it is broken."

"That is why that kind of tea set is no good," said Thelma. "The cups break and the saucers break and the teapot and cream pitcher and sugar bowl break, and then the set is all gone. My tea set has red flowers, and it does not break unless you step on it."

"Well," said Frances, "I am saving up for the other kind."

"How much have you saved up?" said Thelma.

"Two dollars and seventeen cents," said Frances.

"How much does the tea set cost?" said Thelma.

"I don't know," said Frances.

"I am sure they cost a lot," said Thelma. "It will take you a long time to save up all that money."

"I know," said Frances, "and I wish I had a tea set now."

"Maybe I will sell you mine," said Thelma.

"I don't want yours," said Frances. "I want

a real china one with pictures on it in blue."

"I don't think they make them anymore," said Thelma. "I know another girl who saved up for that tea set. Her mother went to every store and could not find one.

Then that girl lost some of her money and spent the rest on candy. She never got the tea set. This is what happens. A lot of girls never do get tea sets. So maybe you won't get one."

"If I buy yours, I will have a tea set," said Frances.

"You said you didn't want it," said Thelma. "And anyhow, I don't want to sell it now."

"Why not?" said Frances.

"Well," said Thelma, "it is a very good tea set. It is plastic that does not break. It has pretty red flowers on it. It has all the cups and saucers. It has the sugar bowl and the cream pitcher and the teapot. It is almost new, and I think it cost a lot of money."

"I have two dollars and seventeen cents,"
said Frances. "That's a lot of money."

"I don't know," said Thelma. "If I sell you
my tea set, then I won't have one anymore."

"We can have tea parties at my house
then," said Frances. "And you can use the
money for a new doll."

"Well, maybe," said Thelma. "Do you have
your money with you?"

"I'll run home for it," said Frances.

"All right," said Thelma. "I will think about
it while you run home for your money."

Frances ran home for her money. When she came back, Thelma said, "I will sell you my tea set."

Frances gave Thelma her money. Thelma gave Frances her tea set.

"No backsies on this," said Thelma.

"All right," said Frances. "No backsies."

Frances went home with her tea set and her dolls, and she sang:

A plastic pot can pour the tea

For my dolls and friends and me

Just as well as china.

Red is just as good as blue.

Plastic cups are all right too,

Just as good as china.

When Frances got home, she showed the
tea set to her little sister Gloria.

"That is a very ugly tea set," said Gloria.

"What's the matter with it?" said Frances.

"It's ugly," said Gloria.

"It's a nice tea set," said Frances.

"It's plastic," said Gloria. "It has red flowers. It's ugly. I like the china kind with the pictures all in blue."

"You can't get that kind anymore," said Frances. "They don't have them in the stores."

"Yes, they do," said Gloria. "They have them now at the candy store. My friend Ida got one yesterday, and she showed it to Thelma. So Thelma knows they have them at the candy store. They cost two dollars and seven cents."

Frances walked slowly to the candy store.

She looked inside, and there was Thelma.

Thelma gave the storekeeper her money.
The storekeeper gave Thelma a china tea set
with pictures all in blue.

Thelma did not see Frances as Frances
walked away.

Frances sang a little song as she walked away:

Now that plastic's what I've got,

Backsies are what there is not.

Mother told me to be careful,

But Thelma better be bewareful.

Frances thought about no backsies all the
way home.

When she got home she put a penny in the plastic sugar bowl of her tea set.

Then she called Thelma on the telephone.

"Hello," said Thelma.

"Hello," said Frances. "This is Frances."

"Remember," said Thelma, "no backsies."

"I remember," said Frances. "But are you sure you really want no backsies?"

"Sure I'm sure," said Thelma.

"You mean I never have to give back the tea set?" said Frances.

"That's right," said Thelma. "You can keep the tea set."

"Can I keep what is in the sugar bowl too?" said Frances.

"What is in the sugar bowl?" said Thelma.

"Never mind," said Frances. "No backsies.

Good-bye." Frances hung up.

Frances waited for the telephone to ring, and when it rang she said, "Hello."

"Hello," said Thelma. "This is Thelma."

"I know," said Frances.

"I just remembered," said Thelma, "I think I had something in the sugar bowl. I think it was a ring. Did you find a ring?"

"No," said Frances. "And I don't have to tell you what is in the sugar bowl because you said no backsies."

"Well," said Thelma, "I just remembered that I put some money in the sugar bowl one time. I think it was some birthday money. I think it was two dollars, or maybe it was five dollars. Did you find money?"

"You said no backsies," said Frances. "So I
don't have to tell you. I don't have to say how
much money is in the sugar bowl."

"Well," said Thelma, "it is my money, and
I want it."

"Do you want backsies?" said Frances.

"Do you want your tea set back and you will give my money back?"

"I can't," said Thelma, "because I used the money for a new tea set. There is only a dime left over. I will give you the new tea set and the dime. The new tea set is the china kind you want. It has pictures all in blue."

"You said they don't make that kind anymore," said Frances.

"This one was very hard to find," said
Thelma. "And I think it was the very last one
in the store."

"All right," said Frances. "Bring it over."

Thelma brought over the china tea set and the
dime, and Frances gave back the plastic tea set.

Then Thelma took the lid off the sugar
bowl and saw the penny.

"That is not a very nice trick to play on a friend," said Thelma.

"No," said Frances, "it is not. And that was not a nice trick you played on me when you sold me your tea set."

"Well," said Thelma, "from now on I will have to be careful when I play with you."

"Being careful is not as much fun as being friends," said Frances. "Do you want to be careful, or do you want to be friends?"

"I want to be friends," said Thelma.

"All right," said Frances. "Then I will give you halfsies on the dime."

Frances and Thelma went to the candy store with the dime. Frances bought bubble gum, and Thelma bought Life Savers.

Then they went back to Frances's house to skip rope. Gloria came out to turn the rope and skip too.

"You and Gloria can skip first," said Frances to Thelma. "I will go last."

Thelma skipped first, then Gloria. Then Frances skipped, and she sang:

One for plastic, two for china,

Three for yours and four for mine-a,

Five for tea and six for cakes,

Seven for elephants, eight for snakes,

Nine's a trip to the candy store,

Then comes ten and ten skips more:

Backsies one, backsies two,

Backsies are no fun to do.

Careful once, careful twice,

Being careful isn't nice.

Being friends is better.

Then Frances and Thelma shared their bubble gum and Life Savers with Gloria.